THE CASE OF THE
Story Rock

ERIC HOGAN & TARA HUNGERFORD

FIREFLY BOOKS

**FOR WILFRED, PARIS
& THEIR GRANDPARENTS.**

Published Under License by Firefly Books Ltd. 2019
Copyright © 2019 Gumboot Kids Media Inc.
Book adaptation and realization © 2019 Firefly Books Ltd.
Photographs © Gumboot Kids Media Inc. unless otherwise
specified on page 32.

This book is based on the popular children's shows *Scout &
the Gumboot Kids*, *Daisy & the Gumboot Kids* and *Jessie & the
Gumboot Kids*.

'GUMBOOT KIDS' is a trademark of Gumboot Kids Media Inc., and
an application for registration is pending in Canada. Trademarks
of Gumboot Kids Media Inc. may not be used without express
permission.

First printing

Library of Congress Control Number: 2019930760

Library and Archives Canada Cataloguing in Publication:
Title: The case of the story rock / Eric Hogan & Tara Hungerford.
Other titles: Scout & the Gumboot Kids (Television program)
Names: Hogan, Eric, 1979- author. | Hungerford, Tara, 1975-
author. | Imagine Create Media, issuing body.
Description: Series statement: A Gumboot Kids nature mystery |
Based on the TV series: Scout & the Gumboot Kids.
Identifiers: Canadiana 20190058269 | ISBN 9780228101918
(hardcover) | ISBN 9780228101925 (softcover)
Subjects: LCSH: Fossils—Juvenile literature.
Classification: LCC QE714.5 .H64 2019 | DDC j560—dc23

Published in the United States by
Firefly Books (U.S.) Inc.
P.O. Box 1338, Ellicott Station
Buffalo, New York 14205

Published in Canada by
Firefly Books Ltd.
50 Staples Avenue, Unit 1
Richmond Hill, Ontario L4B 0A7

Printed in Canada

Canada 🍁 We acknowledge the financial support of the
Government of Canada.

Scout and Daisy are on an expedition. It's dawn and Scout is returning to the campsite after a morning stroll. Daisy is relaxing in a hammock reading a book.

"Morning, Daisy!" says Scout.

"Good morning, Scout."

"What's that you're reading?" asks Scout.

"It's a book about the different animals that live in the desert," replies Daisy.

"Ooh! Sounds interesting!"

"You know, I just came across something very curious on my walk," says Scout.

"Oh really?" says Daisy. "Please, tell me more!"

"Well I found a rock... and it told a story," continues Scout.

"Wait — what? A rock told you a story?" asks Daisy.

"Yes! It told me a story about dinosaurs!" says Scout.

"That's fascinating, Scout! But how can a rock tell you a story about dinosaurs?"

"Well, I thought that could be today's nature mystery," says Scout. "The Case of the Story Rock."

"Great idea! I love solving nature mysteries!" exclaims Daisy.

Scout cracks open his field notes.

"I sketched some clues that will help you solve the mystery," Scout says, pointing to his first drawing.

"Valley — a valley is the low area between two hills," observes Daisy. "There's one over there! Let's go!"

Valley

"Wow! It sure is dry and rocky here," remarks Daisy. "I wonder which one of these rocks told you a story about dinosaurs?"

"Let's check out my field notes for another clue," says Scout.

"A shovel," Daisy remarks as she looks at Scout's field notes.

"Yes," replies Scout as he pulls a shovel from his backpack. "To find a story rock you'll need this shovel, a little patience and a lot of luck."

"I'm up for the challenge!" says Daisy. "But, what kind of a rock are we digging for?"

Shovel

"This next clue will help you," says Scout, pointing to his field notes.

"A spiral!" notes Daisy. "Alright, let's dig!"

Scout and Daisy scan the rocky valley, scraping and digging at the surface.

"Aha! Look what I found!" exclaims Daisy. "It's a spiral-shaped rock."

"Awesome!" says Scout, carefully brushing away the dirt.

Spiral

Daisy leans in with her magnifying glass. "Cool! It's a fossil, isn't it?"

"It sure is!" says Scout.

"Let's head back to the campsite," says Daisy. "I've got a book there that can tell us more."

Back at the campsite, Daisy reads aloud from her book:

Fossils are the remains of ancient animals and plants. They're formed when an animal or plant is buried in mud or sand. Over time they are compressed into rock. It can take thousands, even millions, of years to form a fossil.

"So that means that our fossil could be millions of years old?" asks Daisy.

Plant fossil

Ammonite fossil

Pterodactyl fossil

"That's right," says Scout. "The fossil you unearthed is called an ammonite. It's a sea creature that lived more then 65 million years ago — it was alive when dinosaurs walked the earth!"

"That's amazing," remarks Daisy. "So, if my fossil came from the sea, that means the valley we walked in used to be full of water."

"That's right," says Scout. "Have you solved The Case of the Story Rock yet?"

"Yes, I think so," Daisy nods. "Fossils tell us stories about ancient animals and plants — so the story rock is a fossil!"

"That's right! You *rock*, Daisy!"

"Now let's pause and have a mindful moment," begins Scout. "Every rock tells a story. The next time you pick up a rock, notice the size, shape and color. Notice the texture. How does it feel in your hands? Some rocks are rough, and some rocks are smooth."

"This rock is smooth, and I can see different colors and layers inside," says Daisy. "It's a beautiful rock!"

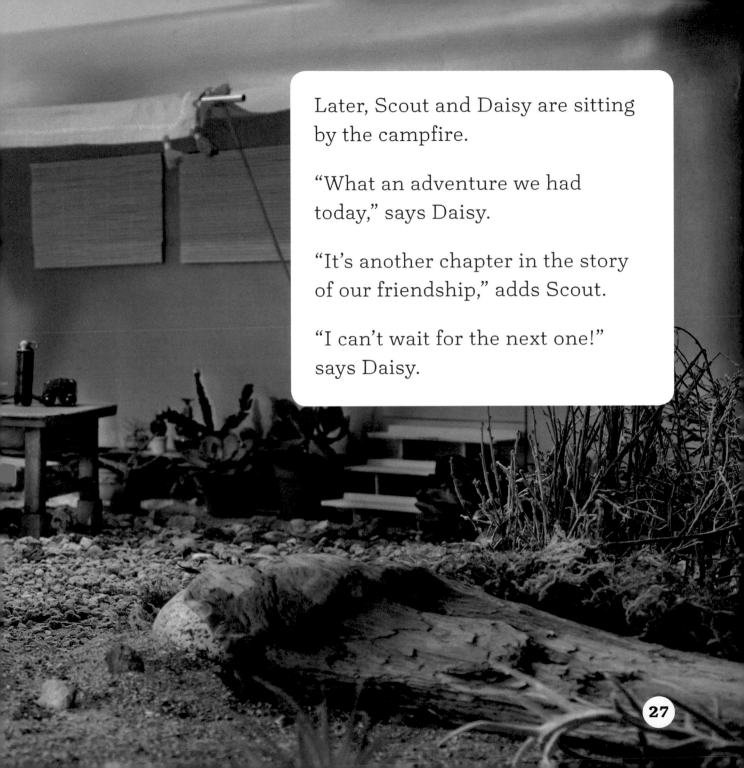

Later, Scout and Daisy are sitting by the campfire.

"What an adventure we had today," says Daisy.

"It's another chapter in the story of our friendship," adds Scout.

"I can't wait for the next one!" says Daisy.

Field Notes

HOW FOSSILS ARE FORMED

Dinosaur fossils are very rare. Many of the fossils discovered were once in watery environments.

First, the dinosaur dies.

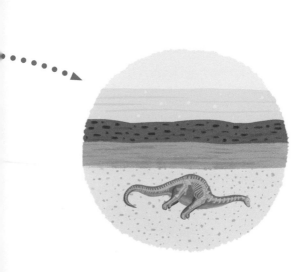

Next, over time, the dinosaur is buried in volcanic ash, mud and silt. Eventually the dinosaur's soft tissues decompose, leaving the hard parts, like bones, behind.

Over time, sediment builds up over the bones and hardens into rock. The bones slowly decay and minerals seep into the bones. This process is called petrification. Petrified bones are the fossils scientists find and use to learn about dinosaurs.

Nature Craft

Daisy was so inspired by fossils, she made some nature impressions. Would you like to make nature impressions?

STEP 1

Head outside and collect some objects with different textures and patterns like a leaf, shell and fallen tree bark.

STEP 2

Gather your craft supplies. You'll need paper, crayons and some tape.

STEP 3

Place a sheet of paper on top of your textured object. To keep the paper in place, tape the four corners down onto your craft table. Then use your crayons and gently rub them back and forth across your paper. Have fun, and remember, there's no right or wrong way to make a nature craft! Creating these works of art is a wonderful way to study the patterns in nature.

TELEVISION SERIES CREDITS
Created by Eric Hogan and Tara Hungerford
Produced by Tracey Mack
Developed for television with Cathy Moss
Music by Jessie Farrell

Television Consultants
Mindfulness: Molly Stewart Lawlor, Ph.D
Zoology: Michelle Tseng, Ph.D
Botany: Loren Rieseberg, Ph.D

BOOK CREDITS
Based on scripts for television by Tara Hungerford,
Cathy Moss and Eric Hogan
Production Design: Eric Hogan and Tara Hungerford
Head of Production: Tracey Mack
Character Animation: Deanna Partridge-David
Graphic Design: Rio Trenaman, Gurjant Singh
Sekhon and Lucas Green
Photography: Sean Cox
Illustration: Kate Jeong

Special thanks to the Gumboot Kids cast and crew,
CBC Kids, Shaw Rocket Fund, Independent Media
Fund, The Bell Fund, Canada Media Fund, Creative
BC, Playology, and our friends and family.

ADDITIONAL PHOTO CREDITS
30 Anick Violette (nature impressions)

Shutterstock.com
20 Albert Russ (bottom fossil), Alice-photo (top
fossil); 21 YuRi Photolife; 30 ND700 (sea shell),
creativestockexchange (crayons), Little Hand
Creations (tape) mama_mia (leaves)

More GUMBOOT KIDS Nature Mysteries

Visit Scout and Daisy
gumbootkids.com